Table of Contents

Chapter 1 – Candy Corn and Costumes

"These donuts aren't in costume, are they?" asked Amy. "Are they going to be as delicious as they look?"

"Have you ever known my mom to make a donut that's not delicious?" Lilly challenged.

"Touché," Amy agreed.

Heather smiled. She was in the kitchen of her shop, Donut Delights, with two of her favorite people in the world: her daughter and her best friend. She was also doing one of her favorite activities: preparing to unveil her newest flavor of donut. Heather always liked to experiment with recipes and set a challenge for herself to create a new tasty treat every week. This challenge ended up being a success for the business too. It not only helped Heather stay creatively satisfied at work, but it also attracted customers who were eager to sample the newest sweets. However, before Heather set the donuts out in her display case, she always had her friends or family act as taste testers.

"Do we get to try it now?" asked Lilly.

"Just let me call some of my assistants over to join us," said Heather. "They should try it too before they learn how to bake them."

She left the kitchen to recruit some more taste testers. The assistants didn't need to be asked twice. Digby, Janae, and Luz hurried toward the counter in the back to try the newest flavor.

Nina graciously agreed to continue watching the register while the others were gone. She looked a tad anxious as she told Heather that she was happy to stay out front anyway because she was hoping that her boyfriend, Nick, who worked in the shop across the street, Sun and Fun Novelties, would come and visit her. Something was bothering him and this, in turn, was bothering her. Heather told her that things would work out and she promised that Nick and Nina could each have an extra donut that afternoon.

Then Heather returned to the kitchen where the others were all looking hungrily at the white, yellow, and orange donuts. She smiled, feeling proud that her creations would inspire such looks of admiration.

"Are you going to let us eat them?" asked Digby. "Or is this a form of Halloween torture where we just get to smell them?"

"If you can guess what they're called you can have one," said Heather mischievously.

"There's something familiar about them," Janae said, bouncing on her toes as she thought.

"Really familiar," said Digby, tapping his chin.

"They remind me of something from when my boys were young," the maternal Luz said. "And something to do with Halloween."

"Is it a candy flavor?" asked Amy.

Heather nodded.

"It's candy corn!" said Lilly. "That's a sweet candy for Halloween, and they are the same colors."

"That's exactly right," said Heather. "And you figured it out before I added the final topping."

Grinning, Heather took of a bowl of candy corn and sprinkled a few on top of each of the donuts on the table in front of her.

"So," Digby said, clearing his throat and kicking the ground. "Does only Lilly get one for guessing the name or do we all get one?"

"You can all have one," said Heather, gesturing for them all to pick one up. "Enjoy the Candy Corn Donut."

"Trick or treat," Amy joked as she picked hers up.

"It's definitely a treat," Lilly said after taking a bite. "This is amazing."

"If I might make a *corny* joke," said Amy. "This is sweeter than *candy*."

"Thank you," said Heather as the others agreed with her friend. "And it's a relatively simple recipe for you all to make. It's a sweet donut base that's covered with even sweeter icing. The only thing you'll need to be careful about is to make sure that the three icing colors stay separate. They should each have one band of color across the donut. I would add them one at a time and give it a few seconds to settle in between. First the yellow, then the orange and then the white icing. And then just sprinkle a few of the candy corns on top."

"I'm glad it's simple," said Digby. "Because I'm sure that we're going to have to bake a lot of them this week. Customers will want to be festive and have them for Halloween."

"Can I have them at my party?" asked Lilly.

"That was my plan," Heather assured her.

They were planning on having an afternoon party on Halloween after school let out where a few of Lilly's new friends from class would come over. They would play some Halloween games and enjoy themselves. However, Heather didn't plan on it being a late night. The guests would leave right before trick-or-treating time. Lilly's best friend in town, Chelsea, was planning on staying though. The two girls planned on collecting candy together.

Heather wondered if this might be the last year that Lilly went trick-or-treating. Next year Lilly would be going to high school. Would she feel too old to ask for candy then? Heather tried not to think about how fast Lilly was growing up and selected a Candy Corn Donut to eat.

"That's great that you're having a party," said Luz. "My husband and I used to go to Halloween parties all the time. But now we like to stay home and hand out candy to the children that come by. I think we're going to be a witch and a warlock again and present the candy in a cauldron."

"I'm going to dress up as a phantom," said Digby. "Like the one from the opera to be theatrical. Not a generic one that haunts stuff."

"That's a fun costume," said Lilly. "I've decided to go as a monster this year. I'm going to be a mummy."

"What about you?" Heather asked Janae.

Her assistant shrugged. "I'm not sure what my Halloween plans are this year yet. And I know I should really figure them out because I only have a few more days. Fire Frank and I are rekindling our relationship but moving slowly. I'm not sure if we're going to do something together or not. What about you, Heather? What are you dressing up as?"

"A zombie again?" asked Luz.

"No," said Heather. "That was just something improvised for a party we went to on short notice. Ryan and I ordered some costumes this year, and the woman who makes costumes for Digby's shows is sewing them."

"Imelda is great," Digby assured them.

"But what is the costume?" asked Luz.

"I'd rather let it be a surprise," said Heather. "It's not a crazy costume, but there's a chance it won't work out. I don't want to hype it up too much."

"Now you're making it mysterious," said Digby.

Heather shrugged. "I guess that's part of the fun of Halloween."

"Will you wear it to work so we can see it?" asked Luz.

"I'd love to wear it," said Heather. "Though it might be a little difficult to bake in."

"Aha!" said Amy. "That's a hint."

"You don't know what it is either?" asked Digby. "I thought you two were besties and told each other everything."

"We are besties," said Heather. "And it's almost everything."

"That's right," Amy said. "She and her husband have been very tight-lipped about their costumes."

"It's really not that exciting," said Heather. "Don't build it up in your mind too much."

"What are you going to dress up as?" Janae asked Amy to try and change the subject for her boss.

"Jamie and I are wearing the same thing we wore to the haunted house Halloween party, which didn't end up being much of a party because somebody died and Heather and I ended up having to work to solve the case. We're dressing up as Cat Burglars again. That's kitty cat thieves."

"It sounds adorable," said Janae.

"I wonder what Nina is doing for Halloween," said Luz. "She doesn't like to be scared."

"Speaking of Nina," said Heather. "Why don't we bring these extra donuts out to the front display case? Then I'll show you the recipe so you can whip up some more today."

They all agreed and carried the Candy Corn Donuts to the front of the shop. However, Amy used the opportunity to try and find out some more about Heather's costume.

"Luz raised an interesting point," said Amy. "Nina doesn't like to be scared. Even around Halloween. Should you wear your costume to work? You don't want to freak her out."

"I don't think she'll find my costume scary," Heather said as she filled the display case with colorful donuts.

"That's another clue," said Amy.

"I know you're a good investigator and that's why you work as my partner," said Heather. "But this isn't something worth inspecting."

Amy shrugged. "Maybe you're right. Maybe I should just focus on Halloween fun. And the scares. Speaking of scares, it looks like one is coming our way."

Amy gestured toward the door where Mr. Rankle was approaching. He was their crotchety neighbor from across the street who owned Sun and

Fun Novelties. He had never been a huge fan of the donut makers and sometimes caused trouble for them.

"Oh no," Nina whispered to them. "Nick sent me a text and told me he didn't think he could get away from the shop. Something is wrong. And now his uncle looks to be in a rage."

Heather agreed with her assessment as Mr. Rankle allowed the door to slam behind him as he entered the shop. He leaned on his cane and glared at those inside.

"Heather!" he yelled. "I have a bone to pick."

Chapter 2 – Riotous Rankle

Heather gulped. She had hoped that she and Mr. Rankle were on better terms now. It was true that he never really liked anyone that he didn't consider a "local" and that Heather and her friends had moved to Key West all the way from Texas. He had been a nuisance for them in the past, doing things from trying to convince potential customers that the donuts made eaters ill, to attempting to have the shop inadvertently violate decoration ordinances. However, after Heather and Amy had helped him with a case or two, some of his venom toward them had died down. He had also seemed a bit mellower after starting to date a woman named Ethel and adopting a cat.

As he stood angrily in the center of Donut Delights, he didn't seem mellow at all. He was practically shaking with rage.

Heather told Lilly to stay with Luz and then walked over to meet Mr. Rankle, taking a glance at her pumpkin themed window display to make sure it didn't contain anything offensive to local ordinances.

"Is everything all right, Mr. Rankle?" Heather asked.

"It most certainly is not," he growled. "I need to talk to you."

As much as Heather didn't want to talk to him, especially when he was in such a state, she didn't want him to disturb the customers in the shop.

"Why don't we have a seat and discuss things?" Heather suggested.

Mr. Rankle gave a curt nod and followed her to a table in the corner. Amy joined her for moral support.

"I suppose you know why I'm here," he said after glowering for a moment.

"Actually, no," said Heather.

"What did we do this time?" asked Amy. "Are the pumpkins in the windows too big? Are you going to insist that the street can only sell a certain amount of candy corn? Are we not supposed to hand out candy to children on Halloween? Are you going to try and put street-wide restrictions on costumes this year?"

"What are you going on about?" asked Mr. Rankle. "I thought you two were supposed to be private investigators. I thought you were supposed to know what was going on."

"Hey! We know what's going on," said Amy. "Just not when it comes to you."

Heather tried to stop a fight and said, "Nina mentioned that something was bothering Nick. Does that have to do with the shop or your troubles?"

"Were you in the kitchen all day?" Mr. Rankle asked accusingly.

"Actually, I was," said Heather. "I was designing my new flavor, the Candy Corn Donut."

"Candy Corn Donut?" Mr. Rankle asked. His eyes lit up for a moment, but then he scowled again.

Mr. Rankle had long maintained that he hated donuts and that Heather's pastries were especially disgusting. However, the investigators had discovered that this was a lie and that his girlfriend, Ethel, would sometimes buy a dozen for him. They all kept up the charade anyway.

"Would you like to try one?" asked Heather.

"No. It sounds repulsive," said Mr. Rankle. "I don't know how you stay in business."

"I wonder the same thing about you," said Amy. "How do you not scare all your customers away?"

"Let's try and get along," said Heather patiently. "Now, Mr. Rankle, can you please come to the point and tell us what you came to say?"

She braced herself to hear what the complaint against the shop would be but was surprised by what he said instead.

"I need your help," he grumbled.

"What?" asked Heather.

"Why?" asked Amy.

"I was vandalized last night," Mr. Rankle said. "My poor shop had eggs thrown all over it. I had Nick

28

come in early and clean it all up. I didn't want anyone to know about it. I don't want others to think of it as a target."

"I guess this ties in with what I was saying about scaring off customers," Amy muttered. "Rankle's charm inspired something else."

"I thought you might have done it at first," said Mr. Rankle. "We never really got along. You are outsiders. You have a kitchen which I'm sure has lots of eggs. And this blonde one here has quite a mouth on her."

Amy glared back at him.

"We wouldn't do something like that," said Heather.

"I realize that," Mr. Rankle said. "And why would you want to waste your materials like that? You'd lose profits. It would be like me throwing snow globes at your place. I might want to, but it's not cost-effective."

"Thanks," said Amy.

"But if it's not you, I don't know who the hooligans are," said Mr. Rankle. "And the police aren't regarding this as a serious matter. They took a statement but gave me the impression that this wasn't something they cared about. A harmless Halloween mischief. Bah! I wish I could give whoever did this a piece of my mind."

"But where do we play into this?" asked Heather.

"Isn't it obvious? I want to hire you as investigators. I want you to find out who egged my shop," he said, tapping his cane on the ground for emphasis.

"I can't believe this is happening," said Amy. "You want us to investigate for you?"

"It would be the neighborly thing to do," said Mr. Rankle. "And I suppose if you did this for me, I could let Nick have Halloween off so he could spend it with your little assistant here. Would that work for payment? Or are you going to pick an old man's pockets?"

"It's not the money I'm worried about," said Heather. "It's what you'll do after we find the culprits."

"I'd love to see them locked up," said Mr. Rankle with glee.

"What if they're children?" asked Heather.

"I'm sure the police have small jail cells too," Mr. Rankle said.

"If we agree to take this case," Heather said seriously, "you're going to have to listen to us about what we feel a just punishment is."

"Fine," Mr. Rankle agreed. "Just find out who they are. And soon. I want this nipped in the bud. I don't want any more vandalism before Halloween."

"All right," Heather said without any enthusiasm. "I guess we're on the case."

Chapter 3 – The Egg Trail

"I can't believe we're doing this," Amy grumbled.

"Which part?" asked Heather. "Investigating for Mr. Rankle? Or bringing the pets?"

"I guess both," said Amy. "How many P.I.s bring a cat on a leash with them?"

Heather laughed. By now she was used to Cupcake, the kitten-soon-to-be-cat, walking on a leash and acting like a dog. Passersby might not think the same thing. Her white mixed-breed dog, Dave, looked more like what people would expect to see, with his leash attached to his collar.

After agreeing to help Mr. Rankle, Heather had asked Lilly what she wanted to do that afternoon. Lilly had said that her mom and Amy should start sleuthing for Mr. Rankle right away so he wouldn't get any crankier. She asked if she could meet up with her friend Chelsea and plan for the party. Heather had called Chelsea's mom, Mrs. Copeland, and she had invited Lilly to come over. (Kelly Copeland was also married to the chief of police and understood when a case popped up suddenly.)

Heather and Lilly had stopped home to pick up Lilly's notebook about her party preparations before going to her friend's house, and Heather had been inspired to bring Dave and Cupcake with her. Dave had helped her with some cases in the past. (Though he was often also responsible for a few disappearing donuts mysteries!) She thought it was possible he might be able to pick up a scent trail. Cupcake didn't want to be left alone and insisted she come as well.

"I'm glad I didn't bring Miss Marshmallow though," said Amy. "She'd hate to get her paws dirty. And I still don't know what to do with Prince. But more than anything I can't believe this case. We're working for Mr. Rankle for Pete's sake! And we usually investigate murders and arsons. Now we're investigating egging."

"It was still a bad thing that these vandals did," said Heather. "Eggs can stain paint and can leave a stench. And I'm not sure Mr. Rankle could have cleaned it all by himself with his bum leg. He's lucky his nephew is so helpful at the shop."

"I don't know. I think Mr. Rankle is still pretty spry," said Amy. "And ornery."

Heather shushed her friend. They were approaching Sun and Fun Novelties with the pets, and she didn't want Mr. Rankle to hear them talking about him.

When they got closer, Heather could see what she had missed earlier when the new recipe was distracting her. The building had recently been washed, but it was not entirely consistent, as if only certain areas of the building required attention. There were also a few small pieces of egg shell on the ground that Nick's broom must have missed.

Amy frowned. "I'm just not sure that I want to catch the people responsible for egging Mr. Rankle's place."

"Come now," said Heather. "How would you feel if they egged our house or Donut Delights?"

Amy mumbled how she'd feel bad about it but how they were much sweeter than Mr. Rankle and how it shouldn't happen to them. Heather decided not to argue with her friend. The best course of action was to find the people responsible for the mischief and then move on.

"All right, Dave, see if you can sniff anything out," Heather instructed. "See if you can tell which way they went."

Dave wagged his tail happily. Heather wasn't sure if he understood anything that she said, but he did start sniffing the ground. Cupcake also put her nose to the ground and copied what Dave was doing.

"It's so hard not to make a copycat joke right now," said Amy.

Heather chuckled, but then she was off following Dave. He started leading them down the street, with Cupcake at his heels, and Heather began to feel excited. Could Dave really lead them toward the culprits? Maybe

they could wrap this case up right
away.

Her enthusiasm began to wane
when she saw that Dave was
leading them toward the
dumpster behind the taco
restaurant.

"Dave, I thought you found
something. Are you just trying to
tell us you want tacos?" asked
Heather.

"That's not a bad idea," said Amy.

Dave barked and wagged his tail.
Heather raised an eyebrow and
wondered if he really had found
something and wasn't just
following his belly. She opened

the dumpster and looked at what was inside.

"Good dog!" she exclaimed.

"Is there something besides taco supplies in there?" asked Amy.

"Egg cartons," Heather said, pointing at them before she knelt down to pet Dave. "Lots and lots of cartons. I think they need to have come from the people who threw the eggs."

"You think it was more than one person?"

"Based on how many cartons are there, I think it would be hard for

one person to carry them all,"
Heather exclaimed.

"Hey! Get away from our
dumpster!" a voice yelled at
them.

Heather turned and saw Juan,
one of the owners of the taco
shop, running toward them. He
stopped as he recognized who it
was.

"Oh, Heather. I didn't know it was
you," he said, putting on a smile.
He and his business partner,
Don, had become huge fans of
her donuts.

"We didn't know you were so protective of your dumpster," said Amy.

"I'm not normally," Juan said. "But I saw some college kids messing with it late last night. We were afraid they were putting a stink bomb or something inside, but it seems like they were just using it to dump their own trash. But with Halloween coming, people could be up to mischief."

"And we think they were at Mr. Rankle's place," said Heather. "That's what was egged."

"Wow," said Juan. "He cleaned it up quick."

"Are you sure they were college kids?" asked Heather.

"Well, one had on a hoodie that said KWCC. I thought that stood for the community college," Juan explained. "A lot of students come by for tacos at one point or another."

Dave barked.

"I think Dave does deserve a taco treat," said Heather. "Could we exchange some tacos now for some Candy Corn Donuts for later?"

"A Candy Corn Donut?" asked Juan. "Sure. That sounds worth

the wait. I'll go get some tacos for you and the animals now."

He returned to the restaurant and Heather looked at the egg cartons some more.

"I know we're much further along than we were a few minutes ago," said Amy. "But there are a lot of college students on the island. Do you think we'll really be able to track these three down?"

"I do," said Heather. "I just saw a price sticker on one of the egg cartons. It's from the Malibu Market in Key West. They have several locations."

"One in Malibu, maybe?" asked Amy.

"I think so. But they're small shops that sell groceries. I bet the one here would remember selling so many eggs at once. And that should point us toward the three college students."

"Easy as pie," said Amy. "Or this time, should I say easy as egg?"

Chapter 4 – The Apology

Heather was proud of how quickly her investigation had worked. After eating some tacos, they went to the Malibu Market and asked about the large egg purchase. The cashier remembered the customers, and after Heather and Amy explained how they often worked with the Key West Police (though usually on more murderous cases), the cashier gave them a name. Heather and Amy easily tracked down the students and convinced them to return to Sun and Fun Novelties.

However, as happy as Heather was about the quick investigation, she wasn't sure what Mr. Rankle would make of it. She knew that Mr. Rankle wanted to see the culprits behind bars. Heather thought that they were being young and stupid and should pay for it in another way.

"How did your search go?" asked Mr. Rankle as Heather and Amy entered the shop.

"We found the boys responsible," said Heather.

"Are they in the slammer?" asked the old man, gripping his cane excitedly.

"They're outside," Heather said. "We thought that instead of involving the police, they could apologize to you and pay for the damage. I think they're willing to do some work around the shop to make up for it too."

"I wouldn't allow them to work here!" cried Mr. Rankle. "Those hooligans!"

"I said when we took the case that you would have to allow us to think of a suitable punishment," said Heather. "We deal with a lot of real monsters in our work when we track down killers. I think what these boys did was destructive and they should have to make it up to you. But they didn't injure anyone. I don't think jail is the answer."

"Bah!" said Mr. Rankle.

"Will you accept their apology and attempts to make it up to you?" asked Heather.

Nick piped up from behind the counter. "I think you really should, Uncle."

"Fine," Mr. Rankle said, though he didn't sound happy about it.

Heather asked Nick to watch Dave and Cupcake, who had been outside with the college students, as she brought the trio inside. The boys were freshmen and looked young. They also looked very embarrassed as they faced Mr. Rankle.

"We're sorry about what we did," said one with freckles.

"It was stupid, and we shouldn't have done it," agreed the boy with sandy-colored hair.

"Yeah," said the third with glasses, sounding a little less sincere.

"Why did you do it?" Mr. Rankle demanded.

"We wanted people to think we were cool on campus," said the freckly one. "We heard about Halloween pranks that seniors did in the past, and we wanted to do something too. We thought we'd start simple. And we found that eggs were cheaper than toilet paper at the market we went to. So we decided to egg a place."

"And why did you decide to vandalize my establishment?" asked Mr. Rankle.

"Because you gave me a hard time when I came here to buy a soda a few days ago," said the one with glasses. "You kept staring at me, and you called me a hooligan."

"It seems like I was a good judge of character," said Mr. Rankle.

"We want to make it up to you," the freckled boy continued. "We saw it was all cleaned up. But we have some money to give you."

"I will accept payment for cleaning supplies," Mr. Rankle said. He leaned on his cane and headed over to the register where he rang up some soap, sponges, and bottles cleaner.

Heather thought that he didn't overcharge them and was happy about that. The boys paid and apologized again.

"We promise not to bother you again," said the blond boy.

"And we won't egg anything again either," said the boy with freckles.

"Right," said the third.

"Back in my day, you would have been caned for what you did. Stunts like that didn't go unpunished. Wasting food and making a mess of people's property," said Mr. Rankle. "You would have been very sorry indeed."

"I guess it's good we're not back in your day," the boy with glasses smirked.

He left the shop looking cocky. His friends followed but looked

like their tails were still between
their legs.

"Again, we're sorry!" the freckled
boy said before running out of the
shop with the others.

Mr. Rankle was shaking his head.

"I hope they'll learn their lesson,"
said Heather.

"Maybe two of them did," said
Amy.

"At least they've had a warning to
stop this behavior," said Heather.
"If they do anything again, there
will be more severe
consequences."

"Well," Mr. Rankle said with an evil grin. "I wouldn't mind that at all."

Chapter 5 – A New Case

The next day, Heather and Amy met in her home kitchen to chat. Lilly was at school, and Heather felt like party preparations were well underway. She was happy with how the egging case had turned out. There was only one thing bothering her: Amy's insistence about finding out her Halloween costume early.

"You have to give me a hint," said Amy. "Come on. One hint."

"Fine," said Heather with a sigh. "I'll give you a hint. The costumes that Ryan and I are wearing are majestic."

"Majestic," said Amy, repeating the word and going into deep thought. Dave and Cupcake stared at her.

"That's right," said Heather.

"Majestic? Are you going as a sunrise? No. You couldn't dress up as a sunrise. Or could you? You could do anything you put your mind to. Would you want to be a sunrise?"

Heather just shook her head. Then her cell phone began ringing. She saw the number belonged to her detective husband.

"It's Ryan."

"Good," said Amy. "Ask him to give me a hint about the costumes too."

However, Heather never did ask him for a hint. Instead, she listened as he told her about a new murder case. He told her that a young man had been bludgeoned to death and asked if Heather and Amy would like to assist with the investigation.

"We'll be right there," Heather assured him after getting the address.

***

As Heather and Amy approached the street address they had been given, Heather couldn't help feeling a sense of déjà vu. They were close to the college campus and market that they had visited the day before.

"I've got a bad feeling about this," said Amy. "And it has nothing to do with Halloween."

Heather nodded.

They continued down the street and toward the alley that Ryan had described. As soon as they were within view, Ryan and his partner, Detective Peters, headed toward them.

"This isn't a fun case," Detective Peters said. "The victim was young."

Heather often thought that Peters was young for his job, and his baby face didn't help with this assumption. However, he had frequently proved himself to be a capable officer.

"He was eighteen years old," Ryan said with a nod. "A freshman at the college."

"What else can you tell us?" asked Heather.

"He was dressed as a superhero," said Ryan. "We think he was coming from a party. His

face was visible though, so we
don't believe this was a case of
mistaken identity. The killer
wanted this person dead."

"Really badly," Peters added.
"The poor kid was hit repeatedly
with a weapon."

Ryan looked away as the medical
examiner beckoned him to come
closer.

"I'll be right back"' said Ryan.
"Will you finish updating them?"

"No problem, partner," said
Peters. "Though there's not much
else to tell you. We're still
searching the area for forensic
evidence. It was a little windy last

night so we're afraid some things might have blown away. But we do know that the victim came here for college. He had his student ID and a driver's license from out of state. His name is Greg Chambers."

"Oh no," said Heather.

"Did you know him?" asked Peters.

"We just met him," said Heather. "Yesterday. He was one of the students who egged Mr. Rankle's store the other night. He wore glasses and was the one who paid for the eggs at the market."

"You're telling me that one night he was egging a shop and the next night he was killed?" asked Peters.

"Looks like he did something else to get him into trouble," said Amy.

"We know two of his friends," said Heather. "They also egged Mr. Rankle's store. Mark and Tom."

"I'm sure we can find them again so you could talk to them," said Amy.

"I think that would be a good idea," said Peters. "Maybe they know if there was a costume party and who else was there. "

"They might also have an idea about who would want to hurt their friend," said Heather with a nod.

"Well, besides Mr. Rankle," Amy joked. "He was still really mad about the egg vandalism even after they apologized. And Greg with the glasses was the rudest of them all."

Ryan returned to the group with a thoughtful look on his face.

"I updated them," said Peters. "But they also updated me. They met the victim yesterday after tracking down who egged Mr. Rankle's store. It seems he was really mad. They also know two of his friends that we could talk to."

"What did you find out?" asked Heather.

"He was killed sometime between ten p.m. and midnight," said Ryan. "The medical examiner needs to complete his autopsy, but he already has an idea of what was used to hit the victim."

"What was it?" asked Amy.

"A long cylindrical object," Ryan explained. "It was about an inch in diameter. It doesn't need to have been too heavy if it was swung with enough force."

"A cylindrical object," Heather said aloud as a thought occurred to her. "Like a man's cane."

"Yes," said Ryan. "That's a great example. The medical examiner used it too."

"Uh oh," said Amy. "I know what she's thinking."

"What's that?" asked Peters.

"I'm thinking of Mr. Rankle's cane," said Heather. "And whether that could be the murder weapon."

Chapter 6 – Reviewing with Rankle

"I know I used to joke about hoping Mr. Rankle would be guilty of some crime so he would be in jail instead of bothering us," said Amy. "But you don't think that he actually killed somebody, do you?"

"Let's see what he has to say first," Heather answered. "Right now everything that makes us suspicious of him is circumstantial."

"I guess so," Amy agreed. "But if we didn't know him, we would think that a man who argued with the victim the day before and who carries around an item that looks

like the murder weapon with him
– well, we'd think he was a prime
suspect. And since we do know
him, I can say that his
temperament doesn't help his
case."

"Let's just talk to him before we
make up our minds," said
Heather.

She parked her car and started
walking toward Sun and Fun
Novelties. She was glad that
Ryan and Detective Peters were
also going to be there with her.
She saw the police cruiser park
and sighed with a bit of relief. Not
looking forward to telling Mr.
Rankle who the vandals were
was nothing compared to how

much she was dreading questioning him like a suspect. She was grateful that detectives were with her.

The four investigators met on the street and then walked into the shop solemnly. Mr. Rankle looked up from behind the register, and Nick stopped arranging postcards to greet them.

"Hello, Nick, Mr. Rankle," Ryan said with a nod of his head. "I'm afraid we're here on official business today."

"Is it about those young hooligans?" Mr. Rankle asked.

"In a way," Amy muttered.

"It must be," Mr. Rankle said, showing some rare enthusiasm and hurrying closer to the officers with his cane. "They've done something else. Revealed their true hoodlum nature. And now you're going to press charges? You want me to be a character witness? I'd enjoy that very much."

"Why do you say that?" asked Peters.

"Because those little ruffians got off too easy," Mr. Rankle said, glaring at Heather. "An apology and payment for a few cleaning supplies after vandalizing my business. Bah! They need a real punishment. And I'll be happy if I'm involved in giving it to them."

"What sort of punishment do you believe they deserve?" asked Ryan.

Heather bit her lip. She knew Mr. Rankle was talking himself deeper and deeper into trouble, but if he really was the killer, she shouldn't interrupt the police and stop them from doing their jobs.

"I'd love to box them about the ears," said Mr. Rankle with a touch of glee. "Or some hard labor. But I'll settle for some jail time or community service."

"And you met the people who egged your business yesterday?" asked Ryan.

"That's right," said Mr. Rankle. "And I knew they were trouble. Especially the boy with glasses. His apology was the most insincere."

The investigators looked at one another. Nick walked over to them, starting to look concerned.

"Do you mind if we look at your cane?" asked Ryan.

Mr. Rankle gripped his cane protectively. However, then he grudgingly nodded. He leaned on his nephew as he handed it over.

"But why do you want to see it?" he asked as Ryan examined it.

Ryan didn't answer. Instead, he handed it over to Heather. As the scent reached her nose, she frowned.

"It smells like bleach," said Heather.

"That's right," said Mr. Rankle. "With all the cleaning supplies I kept from those boy's apology, I used some to spruce up my cane. It does travel with me everywhere. I wanted to make it clean."

Heather knew that bleach could certainly make a cane clean. It could also ruin blood traces on an item. Had Mr. Rankle really cleaned off the cane to hide the evidence of his crime?

"And you decided to do this yesterday?" asked Amy.

"Because I had the cleaning supplies," said Mr. Rankle, eyeing them all suspiciously.

"Can you tell us where you were last night?" asked Detective Peters. "Specifically between 10 p.m. and midnight?"

"Where do you think I was?" Mr. Rankle snapped, grabbing his cane back. "I was home. Watching TV. Though there is nothing good on these days. And then I went to bed. I'm a working man. I need to get my rest in order to get to the shop on time. And I hoped it wouldn't be vandalized again last night. Luckily, they must have run out of eggs."

"Was anyone with you?" asked Heather. "Maybe Ethel was visiting? Or Nick?"

"It was just the cat and me," said Mr. Rankle.

"I was catching a late movie at the theater with Nina," said Nick. "But what is this all about?"

"Murder," said Amy ominously.

"Oh, not again," Mr. Rankle groaned. "Ever since you moved here, there's been a crime wave!"

"I don't think that's fair to say," said Heather. "Maybe you're just hearing about the cases more now because your neighbors are assisting to find those responsible for the crimes."

"Bah," Mr. Rankle replied. "Now who died this time?"

"Greg Chambers," said Ryan. "One of the college students who egged your business."

Mr. Rankle opened his mouth in shock and then turned on Heather. "How dare you! You tricked me. You tried to make me say bad things about those hooligans so the police would think I killed him. I never killed anyone! Though I am tempted now."

"Easy does it," Nick said to his uncle before appealing to the investigators. "You can't really think that he did it. We were upset by the egging, but we wouldn't kill anyone because of it. And they had already apologized."

"The weapon that killed the boy is consistent with the size of this cane," said Ryan. "We had to ask where you were."

Heather was glad that Nick had an alibi with Nina at the movies, so her assistant's boyfriend wouldn't be considered a serious suspect. She was less certain that Mr. Rankle would be leaving the suspect list.

"Do you mind if we test this cane at the lab?" Detective Peters asked.

"I certainly do!" said Mr. Rankle. "What am I supposed to walk around on? Get yourself a warrant if you want to see it."

"I don't think my uncle could have used this cane as a weapon," said Nick. "He needs it to support himself and walk."

"The medical examiner doesn't think much strength was needed," said Peters.

"I didn't kill anyone," Mr. Rankle repeated. "And I think you should all leave my shop now."

"We will," said Ryan. "But you shouldn't leave town, Mr. Rankle."

"I won't," Mr. Rankle replied. "This is my town. I won't leave. Maybe some others should!"

Heather headed toward the door with the other investigators. She was happy to get away from Mr. Rankle's rage. This was going to be a difficult case.

Chapter 7 – Candy Corn Conference

That afternoon, Heather found herself elbow-deep in papier-mâché. She and Lilly were making a monster piñata for the Halloween party. They planned on filling it with lots of candy that the partygoers could knock out of the green monster and enjoy.

There was a knock at the front door, and Dave began barking.

"Come in!" Heather called.

A moment later, Amy and Jamie entered along with a group of animals. Dave and Cupcake were bouncing around, happy to see their friends. Miss Marshmallow,

Amy's dog, was standing to the side, looking daintily aloof, while Prince, the miniature black poodle that they were watching, wagged his tail.

"I bet they all think we're cooking donuts," said Heather. "But much to the pups' disappointment, we're just working with soggy, sticky paper."

"It's looking pretty good though," said Amy. "When I got your text that you were having artistic trouble, I feared the worst. I think you just need to even out one of the monster's claws and it will look fearsome."

"Thanks, Amy," said Lilly. "We knew there was something off about it."

Amy joined them at the table and began helping by adding strips of paper to the piñata. Jamie entertained the animals as they worked.

"Did you come to hear if there were any updates about the case, Jamie?" Heather asked. "I'm afraid there aren't any. Ryan and Peters are looking at getting a warrant to test Mr. Rankle's cane. Based on what we know so far, the chief thinks Mr. Rankle is the most likely suspect."

"The chief must have met him," Amy joked.

"I don't know if he did it or not," said Heather. "But refusing to test the cane doesn't look good for him."

"I was interested in the case after Amy mentioned it," said Jamie. "But that's not really why I'm here."

"I do have some Candy Corn Donuts in the kitchen," Heather said. "But I can't get them while my hands are this dirty."

"No," said Jamie. "I mean, yes. I would love to have some donuts. Especially Candy Corn Donuts.

They sound great for the holiday. Perfect for Halloween. But it's also because of Halloween that I'm here. And because of Amy. She's really curious about what you're dressing up as on the thirty-first, and she recruited me to help find out."

"I can't believe you brought in reinforcements after I told you to drop it," said Heather.

"I can't help it," said Amy. "Your hint wasn't good enough to figure out what it was."

Heather sighed. "I thought it was a good hint."

"We're not asking for any more hints," said Jamie quickly. "But can I make a couple of guesses and if I'm right you'll tell me?"

"I guess so," said Heather. He *was* keeping the pets calm while they worked on the piñata.

"Okay," Jamie said, rubbing his hands together. "What about werewolves?"

"After all the hair we saw stuck on our friend Rudolph Rodney after the last party?" asked Heather. "No way."

"What about a headless horseman?" asked Jamie.

"That's not a bad guess," said Heather. "Because we are going on that trip to Sleepy Hollow soon for their event that is in need of some delightful donuts the weekend after Halloween. But that's not the costume we're wearing this year."

"Remember," Amy said. "She told me it was majestic."

"Then, you're going as birds of some sort?" asked Jamie. "Their flight is majestic!"

Heather shook her head. She was saved listening to any more guesses by another knock at the door. Since Jamie was the only one whose hands weren't sticky with papier-mâché, he went to answer the door.

A moment later, he brought Nick inside. Nick bent down to pet the three animals eager to say hello. Miss Marshmallow didn't deign to take part in the greetings. Then he looked at Heather.

"Heather, my uncle is really upset about what happened," he began.

"And he probably blames us," said Amy.

"He doesn't like being accused of murder," said Nick. "And I don't believe that he did it. Even if he doesn't have an alibi, it just doesn't seem like something he would do. He yells and complains. He doesn't beat people up. And he doesn't kill people."

"If he would let Ryan test the cane more thoroughly, we could exonerate him," said Heather.

"I think he's too angry at being accused to agree to it. His pride is hurt. But that doesn't mean that he is guilty," said Nick. "I know you've solved a ton of cases before. Nina has told me about so many of them, and she's really proud of you. I know you're great investigators. Please say that you'll take another look at this case. See if you can find out who really did this."

Heather looked at his face. Nick looked earnest and worried. It was clear that he didn't think Mr. Rankle was a killer. Heather thought about it too. She had considered Mr. Rankle to be someone who caused trouble indirectly. He yelled a lot, but she had never seen him be violent.

He was also their neighbor on the street. Regardless of her feelings toward him, she owed it to him to look more thoroughly at the case.

"Okay," Heather said. "We won't wait for Ryan and Peters to get the warrant and test the cane. We'll start looking at other alternatives right away. Or…right

92

after we finish putting together
this monster piñata."

Chapter 8 – College

After finishing the piñata, Heather was true to her word. She jumped right into her investigation. She did take some time to see if her senior neighbors, Eva and Leila, would keep an eye on Lilly while she was away sleuthing. Then she and Amy headed toward the local college.

"I feel like college has changed since my day," Amy said, looking at the campus as they arrived. "There are a lot more cell phones and murder than when I went to art school."

Heather nodded. "I think this is a good place to start though. We'll talk to Mark and Tom again and see if they knew anything about Greg Chambers's activities that night."

"And if anyone besides Mr. Rankle wanted to kill him," Amy agreed.

They followed the same route they had the last time they came to the campus to talk about the egging. Heather noticed that the alleyway where Greg Chambers had been found was within walking distance of the school and pointed this out to her friend.

"And since he was in costume, he was most likely leaving an on-campus Halloween party," said

Amy. "But where was he heading?"

"I hope his friends might know," said Heather.

They continued walking across the quad. The campus was not large, but it had a few buildings of classrooms and dorms. She was sure that all the buildings had a lovely view of the beach from their higher windows and wondered whether that would be a distraction to the students.

As she knocked on Mark Erickson's door, she saw that Greg's death had become very distracting for his friends. The freckly Tom was also in the room, and they both greeted the investigators in a very lackluster way.

They allowed them to enter the room as soon as the P.I.s asked. However, seating was limited. They all found themselves sinking into beanbag chairs.

"I hope the guy from Sun and Fun Novelties doesn't want anything else from us," said Mark, pushing his sandy-colored hair away from his face. "I can't focus on that again. Knowing Greg is dead has all my attention."

"We were trying to play some video games to cheer us up," said Tom. "But it didn't work. We can't focus. And we can't believe Greg is dead. If the business owner wants us to do some work for him, please ask him to wait a few days. We're having trouble coming to terms with this murder."

"It's because of the murder that we're here," said Heather.

"That's right," said Amy. "We don't just track down people who throw eggs at buildings. We also catch killers."

"And we'd like to ask you some questions because you were friends with Greg Chambers," said Heather.

"We'll tell you anything you want to know," said Tom. "We want to help."

"That's right," said Mark, though he sounded a bit more reticent.

"How long have you known Greg Chambers?" asked Heather.

"We met him at the orientation over the summer," said Tom. "Our rooms are all in the same wing. We became friends almost instantly."

"We were supposed to be friends forever," said Mark sadly.

"You must miss him terribly," said Heather sympathetically. She wanted to reach out and pat his hand but had trouble sitting up in the beanbag.

"We'd like to find out who did this to him," said Amy. "Do you have any ideas?"

"Maybe that store owner?" said Mark. "He did seem really mad."

"You're right," said Tom. "I didn't think of it before. But that has to be who did it."

"I wonder if we'll get our money back from the cleaning supplies if they catch him as the killer," said Mark.

"That is one possible suspect," said Heather. "But we're looking for others as well."

"Did you commit any other Halloween mischief to make people mad at you?" asked Amy. She crossed her arms to look more authoritative but ended up sinking further into her beanbag seat.

Tom and Mark exchanged a look. Tom bit his lip, but Mark answered.

"No. We didn't do anything that would have gotten Greg killed. And we learned our lesson after the novelty shop guy yelled at us.

And I bet he was the one who did it to Greg."

"Where were you both last night?" asked Heather. "Between ten and midnight?"

"We were together," said Tom.

"That's right," said Mark. "And we got hungry for a late night snack. We went to the twenty-four-hour dining hall for some pizza. And we were there for a while just chilling. It must have been until after midnight when we realized it was late. And I'm sure other people saw us there."

Tom nodded a freckled face.

"And Greg wasn't with you?" asked Heather.

"He went to a Halloween party," said Tom.

"Why didn't you?" asked Amy.

"Well, Greg was going with his girlfriend, Georgia," said Mark. "And we don't have girlfriends right now. And we didn't really feel like partying that night. We just hung out together."

"Greg dressed up as a superhero?" asked Heather.

"That's right," said Tom. "He showed us before he left with Georgia. He wasn't wearing a mask though because of his glasses. He didn't think he needed one though."

"So, he definitely wasn't killed as a case of mistaken identity," Heather said quietly to Amy. "The mask wasn't taken by the killer."

Amy nodded and then asked, "Do you know anyone else who would have wanted to hurt Greg? Maybe a super villain? Or some other enemy?"

"Well, the only person I know that had a problem with Greg was Professor Adler," said Tom. "He seemed to really hate him."

"Any particular reason?" asked
Heather.

Mark and Tom shrugged.

"He's the only enemy I can think
of," said Tom.

"Though his girlfriend could be
annoying too," said Mark.

"That's why we didn't want to go
to the party," said Tom. "And they
were arguing some too."

"But if the killer wasn't that shop
owner," said Mark. "Then,
Professor Adler is who you want
to talk to."

"Thank you," said Heather, struggling to rise from the beanbag. "He is exactly who I would like to speak with."

Chapter 9 – Other Suspects

Heather was feeling happy that they had finally found a suspect other than Mr. Rankle to interview. However, the joy was short-lived because as soon as they reached Professor Adler's office, they saw that he was not inside.

A note taped to the door informed students that he was away for a conference that day and he wouldn't return until tomorrow. However, this did not mean there was an excuse to not turn in homework electronically as assigned.

"I wonder if he was at the conference or traveling to it at the time that Greg Chambers was killed," said Heather.

"We'll just have to ask him about it when he gets back," said Amy. "And we can see how many students tried not to turn in their homework."

Heather nodded. This might be a delay in their investigation, but it wouldn't stop them. They would just have to talk to Professor Adler when he returned to see if he had a motive and alibi.

"What do you want to do now?' asked Amy. "We are on a college campus. Want to find someone strumming a guitar in a hallway and listen?"

"Actually," said Heather as the thought came to her. "I think there's someone else I'd like to talk to besides the professor."

"Who?"

"The girlfriend, Georgia." Heather explained, "If she and Greg were really fighting, then she could be a suspect in the murder. If not, she still might know more about him leaving the party than we know now."

"Good idea," said Amy. "And it was better than my second idea of starting a game of ultimate Frisbee in the quad."

***

"You're the police?" Georgia asked after Heather and Amy had tracked her down and found her room. She leaned against the door and watched them.

"We're not the police, but we do work with them often," Heather explained. "We're private investigators looking into Greg Chambers's death."

"Sometimes the detectives think it's easier for a girlfriend to talk to other women," Amy said. She was making it up, but it worked for Georgia.

"I guess you're right," Georgia said, letting them in and allowing them to sit on her two chairs. She sat on the edge of her bed. "I wouldn't like to talk to a scary police officer after something so terrible happened to me. You two seem nice."

"Thanks," Amy said with a smile.

"But we will have to ask you some difficult questions," said Heather. "We're trying to understand how Greg Chambers ended up where he was when he was killed."

Georgia nodded. "I bet you know that Greg and I went to a party last night."

"A costume party where Greg was a superhero," said Heather.

"Did you dress up too?" asked Amy, becoming excited for a moment. "What did you go as?"

"I was a witch," said Georgia.

"That's not majestic," Amy muttered, and Heather realized that she had been fishing for ideas about what to guess Heather was dressing up as for Halloween.

"It was supposed to be scary," said Georgia. She gestured to a black costume on a hanger with a white wig and hat next to it. "And

I think it was a pretty good costume. Of course, I had to wash it today because someone spilled a drink on me. That was gross."

"Was Greg Chambers with you when that happened?" asked Heather.

"Yes," Georgia replied. She looked down at the ground sadly.

"What is it?" asked Heather.

"That was the last time I saw him," said Georgia. "We went to the party together. We were having a pretty good time. But then someone spilled that drink on me. I wanted to go home, but he wanted to keep partying. I thought he wasn't being a good boyfriend and we had a fight. We both stormed off. I went home to my room. I showered and cried. And then I felt really bad about our fight the next day when I heard he had been killed. I can't believe that was the last thing I said to him."

"Do you know what time this fight was?" asked Heather.

"I guess around ten thirty," said Georgia. "Greg wanted to stay until midnight because he thought there would be something cool that happened. But I was wet and angry. I didn't want to stay there for over an hour."

"You said he stormed off," said Heather. "Do you know where he went?"

"I thought he was just moving away from me," said Georgia. "Because our fight was about staying at the party. I figured he stayed after I left."

"Do you know who else was at the party?" asked Heather. "Who might have seen him leave?"

Georgia shrugged. "There were a lot of people from school there, but everyone was in costume. I don't know exactly who was there."

"Did anyone see you leave or return to your room?" asked Heather.

"I'm not sure," Georgia replied. "But I wasn't being quiet. One of the other girls on the floor might have heard me come home."

"And do you have any idea why Greg could have gone to that alley?" asked Heather.

"None," said Georgia. "I thought he was at the party."

Heather nodded. There was one more line of questioning she needed to ask.

"Do you know anyone who would have wanted to hurt your boyfriend?" asked Heather. "Any suspicions about who could have done this?"

"I know he had some troubles with one professor. A psychology teacher named Adler," Georgia said thoughtfully. "But he also had some trouble with a store owner recently. Some novelty shop in town. Greg made it sound like the guy really hated his guts. Maybe he was the one who killed him."

"Unfortunately, that may be true," said Heather.

Chapter 10 – Ethel's Plea

After an already busy day, Heather returned to Donut Delights to help it close down for the night. The motion of cleaning the counters helped her to think, and she enjoyed seeing the smiles on her employees' faces when she let them eat the few remaining donuts of the day.

"Just don't touch the donuts in the box by my purse," said Heather. "I need to bring some of the Candy Corn Donuts home to my babysitters. If I know Eva and Leila, they'll have finished all the pre-party prep with Lilly before I get home without my asking them to. And then I'll need something to thank them with."

Digby made a dramatic sigh as a joke that they were the donuts he really wanted. Then, he joined Janae and Luz cleaning up while Nina walked up to Heather.

"Have you had any luck with the case?"

"We've spoken to a few people, but we haven't had a big break yet," Heather replied.

"I know Nick is worried about Mr. Rankle," said Nina. "And even if Mr. Rankle does scare me, I care about him because Nick does."

"I know the feeling," said Heather. "Some days I think of him like an enemy and others like a neighbor."

"I hope he didn't do it."

"Whoever did it, we'll find them," Heather assured her. "And I want to thank you for your help so far."

"You mean the movie ticket stubs?" asked Nina.

"That's right. Of course, I believed you when you said that you were with Nick at the time of the murder. But having the movie stubs gives us some physical evidence for this alibi as well," said Heather. "And Nick has the same motive that Mr. Rankle would have for committing the murder."

"Do you think one of the victim's friends could have done it?" asked Nina. "They were part of the egg throwing together. Maybe they fought about it after they were caught."

"It's possible," said Heather. "They told us they were together at the time of the murder at the twenty-four-hour dining hall. We'll have to see if we can find some other witnesses to verify it."

"Unless they got a ticket," Nina teased.

"We also spoke to the girlfriend," said Heather. "She claims to have left the party and gone to her room when her witch costume had liquid spilled on it. She helped narrow down the time of death because she told us Greg was still alive at ten thirty. But there's another suspect that Amy and I will talk to tomorrow."

"Someone is trying to get in," Janae reported as a woman approached the shop door.

"I should have turned off the front lights earlier," said Heather. "Tell her we're closed, but she can have some of the extra donuts from closing free of charge."

"You're trying to give my donuts away?" Digby accused playfully.

Heather laughed. However, when she heard a commotion at the door, she sent her attention that way. It seemed the woman did not take the offer of donuts and was forcing her way inside. But as she came into view better, Heather could see that she knew the woman. It was Ethel Thornbrush, Mr. Rankle's lady friend.

"Heather, please tell me that you don't consider my beau a murder suspect," she pleaded as she made her way into the center of Donut Delights and grabbed Heather's arm.

"We're still investigating the murder," Heather said. "But he hasn't been exonerated as a suspect yet."

"This isn't some sort of Halloween trick you've all cooked up?" Ethel asked.

"I'm afraid not."

"Oh dear," Ethel replied. "I know that you considered me a suspect in a murder once."

"Briefly," Heather said with a small smile. She had tracked down Ethel as a small-time gambler in one of her investigations and had thought of her as a suspect before she learned more about the woman. She was frail in stature and sweet in nature – though she did love bingo and the pony races.

"That was before you knew me though," said Ethel. "But you know him. You shouldn't think of him as a real suspect. I know he can be prickly at times."

"Understatement," Digby said, hiding the word as a pretend cough.

"But he's a good man. He wouldn't kill anyone," Ethel finished.

"I have to go where the evidence leads," said Heather. "And Mr. Rankle was upset with the victim. And Greg Chambers was killed with an object like a cane. And Mr. Rankle had just bleached his."

"But you don't know for certain it was a cane. Let alone his," said Ethel. "What if it was something else round? Like a pipe. Or a mop."

"That might be the case," Heather admitted. "And we are looking into it. I am taking this case seriously. I even questioned Nina to make sure that Nick couldn't be a suspect. I am looking at all possibilities. I'm not trying to railroad Mr. Rankle."

Ethel took a deep breath. "I believe you. I think he might suspect that you're out to get him, but I know better. You're a kind woman who helped me get out of my house and meet the man of my dreams."

"The man of her dreams?" Digby whispered incredulously.

"I just hate seeing him so angry and sad," said Ethel. "He's in terrible spirits, and he was just starting to be in a happy mood. We had even made Halloween plans. We were going to go on a sunset cruise."

Heather kept her thoughts on Halloween cruises to herself because the one that she had been on had resulted in a man being murdered and her friends getting into danger as they tried to catch the culprit.

"And we were going to dress as Gomez and Morticia Addams," said Ethel.

"Then, I'm just going to have to get this case solved in the next two days," said Heather.

If Mr. Rankle was innocent, she didn't want his plans and happy mood to disappear. She also really wanted to see him in costume! Of course, this didn't leave her much time to get to the bottom of things.

Chapter 11 – The Professor in the Office with a Cane

The next morning, Heather and Amy knocked on Professor Adler's office door. They heard an exasperated sigh from inside the room, and then a voice drawled, "I posted that there were no excuses not to turn in the assignment."

"We're not students," Amy replied with attitude. "We're with the police."

The door quickly opened, and they were met by a man with horn-rimmed glasses and long graying hair. He stared at them up and down.

"You don't look like police officers," he said haughtily.

"We're not," said Heather. "But we work with them. And we're investigating the death of one of your students. Would you mind answering a few questions?"

"I am extraordinarily busy, having just returned from a conference," he said. "But I suppose considering the unusual circumstances, I can speak with you. I've only just heard about the tragedy upon my return."

He returned to his office, and the investigators followed him. They sat in the two hard and uncomfortable chairs in front of his desk. Professor Adler leaned back in his cushioned office chair.

"It was Greg Chambers who died, correct?" asked the professor. "The rumor mill here isn't always reliable, but I would hope they would have information as important as this accurate."

"Yes. Greg Chambers was found dead not far from campus," said Heather. "He was killed sometime between ten-thirty and midnight."

"It's a terrible thing that happened," said Professor Adler. "We've never had this happen to one of our students before. But I can't say I'm completely surprised."

"Why is that?" asked Heather.

"I am an expert in psychology," he replied. "I know of the depths of man's depravity. The human mind can be terrifying. However, I know all this in an academic sense. The mind of a murderer would be a fascinating thing to study."

"I'm not sure Greg Chambers would agree," said Amy.

"Can you tell us anything about him?" asked Heather. "He was in your class?"

"Yes. He was in my Introduction to Psychology class," Professor

Adler said. "I can't tell you much about him though, I'm afraid. He wasn't the most studious of my pupils. He didn't attend all my lectures."

"We heard from some other students that the two of you didn't get along," said Amy.

"Fascinating," replied the professor. "And I suppose now you consider me a suspect in the boy's death? I imagine the mind of an investigator might also be interesting to study. It tries to be so logical, but is limited by what is presented before it."

"Why don't you tell us about the victim instead of studying us?" Heather suggested.

"Or I'll give you a fist to study," Amy muttered.

"Very well. Though the notion that I could have harmed one of my students is absurd, I will honor your investigation. I'll tell you about my time with Greg Chambers. Yes, he was troublesome. When he did come to class, he would either make jokes or fall asleep. It was annoying and disrespectful to me. Usually, I would be content to let the student fail. However, in this case, I attempted something different. And I think this is what the other students are referring to."

"What did you do?" Heather asked.

"I tried to employ some psychological techniques to motivate the boy. To see if he would rise to my challenge and become more academic. Unfortunately, some of the other students might have incorrectly viewed it as me insulting the boy before them all."

Amy tilted her head thoughtfully. "It sounds more to me like you lost your temper in the classroom."

"No, no. Not at all. I was employing some of the very latest psychological tools for dealing with unruly students."

Heather allowed the back and forth between the other two to continue a little longer. Amy was baiting him by saying he was just covering up yelling at someone and the professor insisted that he was using the latest techniques. Heather looked around the room as she listened to how it was possible for the professor to lose his temper.

The office was filled with books, and awards adorned the wall. There were some filing cabinets in the corner. There was also a coat rack near the door that Heather had not seen previously because her back was toward it. A jacket was hanging off it, but that wasn't what caught Heather's attention. An ornate cane was leaning against the rack.

"Is that your cane?" Heather asked, interrupting the escalating argument between the other two.

"Why, yes it is," Professor Adler said, rising and walking over to pick it up. "It is lovely, isn't it?"

"Why do you need a cane?" asked Amy. "You look like you can walk fine on your own."

"A psychological trick," Professor Adler explained. "Carrying it around makes me appear more dignified and garners more respect from my peers. And this cane is really an exquisite one. Behold the detail work. I couldn't resist getting it when I attended a conference in Vienna a few years ago."

"And you always walk with it?" asked Heather.

"Usually," he replied. "One wants to be greeted with respect most everywhere."

"Would you allow us to borrow it?" asked Heather. "Just for a short while. It might help with our investigation."

"I'm afraid I can't allow that," Professor Adler said, returning the cane to its location. "It's far too valuable for me to lend out. It's very expensive, you know. And now, if there's nothing else – I do have work to attend to. Molding the minds of young students."

"There is one more thing," Heather said as she was herded toward the door. "You never told us where you were at the time of the murder. Were you traveling to the conference or in town?"

"I suppose I was still in town," Professor Adler said. "But I must have been getting my rest that night in preparation for travel. I was home with my wife."

"Thank you for your time," Heather began to say, but he had shut the door as soon as the investigators were pushed out.

Heather and Amy glared at the closed door.

"I wish I could give him a piece of my *mind*," said Amy.

Chapter 12 – Campus Questions

"What do you think of him?" Heather asked as she and Amy started walking around campus.

"I think Professor Adler is pompous and a bully. *He* also thinks he's the greatest thing since sliced bread."

Heather nodded. "I know of many good psychologists and psychiatrists who conduct studies or who help people through difficult times."

"Sure," Amy agreed. "Jamie started seeing a therapist after he had trouble coming to terms with that stalker situation. The therapist was really great and helped him realize that it wasn't his fault that someone chose him as a target. Jamie says it really helped him recover to have a professional there for support."

"But I don't feel like Professor Adler is the same sort of person. He seems to want to use his subject for, if I might use a psychology term, self-aggrandizing."

"And he didn't like Greg Chambers challenging him in class," said Amy.

"Right," said Heather. "When I asked what you thought of him, I really meant whether you thought he could be the killer."

"I wouldn't write him off," said Amy. "It's clear he and Greg rubbed each other the wrong way. And maybe the professor wanted a permanent way to get him out of class."

"And he did have that cane," said Heather with a nod. "That could be the murder weapon that was used."

"What should we do now?" asked Amy. "Talk to the wife?"

"I would normally say so, but I'm pretty certain she will back up her husband's alibi of being home that night. We might as well finish what else we wanted to do on campus before we speak to her." Then, she said thoughtfully, "Maybe we should ask Ryan and Peters to talk to her. She might be less willing to lie to the police about an alibi than to us."

"Sounds like a plan," said Amy. "But what do we still need to do on campus? I wasn't planning on trying any of the dining hall food when I know there are donuts at home for me."

"I think we should talk to some girls on Georgia's floor and see if they confirm what she told us."

"Great," said Amy. "And then, donuts."

***

Heather and Amy returned to the dorm floor where Georgia lived and saw two girls sitting in the social area, making bracelets out of beads.

"Hello. I'm Heather Shepherd, and this is Amy Givens. You might have heard that we're assisting the police to find out what happened to Greg Chambers. Do you mind if we talk to you?"

"No problem," said the blonde girl. "I'm Casey, and this is Jess."

"But do you mind if we keep making this jewelry?" asked Jess. "We need them for a fundraiser, and we're running behind."

"I'll help you make them while we talk," Amy offered. "I usually paint or make sculptures, but I'm sure I could create some jewelry too."

The girls scooted over so Amy and Heather could sit down. Amy started picking up beads and making bracelets. Heather focused on her questions.

"Did you know Greg Chambers?"

"Not very well," said Casey. "I have a psych class with him, but he doesn't show up all the time. Not that I blame him after the way Professor Adler berated him in front of everyone. But I didn't really talk to Greg when he was there."

"He was dating someone on our floor," said Jess. "And he lives in the building, so I've seen him around."

"We did want to ask you about his girlfriend," said Heather.

"Georgia Giffin," said Casey with a nod. "She can be a bit territorial. But she was crazy about Greg."

"We did hear them fighting before," Jess pointed out.

"I guess so. But Greg could rub anyone the wrong way. He got under Professor Adler's skin. And he was fighting with his friends the other day too."

"Who was that?" asked Heather.

"His two friends that he's normally with." Casey bit her lip. "What were their names? Mike and Tim?"

"Mark and Tom," said Jess. "They were fighting about going to a Halloween party. I guess Greg wanted to go with Georgia and the guys wanted him to do

149

something else with them. I'm not completely sure. They were headed toward their floor at the time."

"That's interesting," said Heather. "You two didn't happen to go to that Halloween party, did you?"

"No," said Jess. "We were too busy."

"We need to make five thousand of these bead bracelets before Halloween to sell at the Monster Mash. The proceeds are going to charity so we can't let them down," Casey agreed.

"We were making them that night," said Jess.

"So, you were up late?" asked Heather. "Did you happen to see Georgia come back to the dorm?"

"Yeah. It was a little after ten-thirty, I guess," said Casey. "She was complaining about a spill on her costume. She was pretty upset. But she just stormed past me."

"I think I was getting more supplies from my room when she came back," said Jess. "I did see her when she and Greg left though. She was dressed as a witch, ready to fly off into the night."

"I just have one more question," said Heather. "Do you know anyone who would have wanted to harm Greg Chambers?"

The girls shook their heads.

"I'm sorry," said Casey. "I wish we could be more help."

"You've already been very helpful," Heather assured them. "Come on, Amy. We've got some more work to do."

"But I'm not finished with my bracelet!"

Chapter 13 – The Dining Hall

Heather and Amy walked across campus, discussing what they had learned, and sporting a bracelet that Amy had created and then bought for charity.

"That was fun," said Amy. "I wish more of our witness questionings could go like that."

"And we did learn some new information too," said Heather. "Georgia's story and timeframe seem to be confirmed and so was Professor Adler's behavior in class. But we know now that Greg also argued with his friends about going to the party."

"Sometimes friends do just argue about silly things," said Amy. "Like who took the last donut in the morning."

Heather rolled her eyes. "I told you I counted them this morning and I know there was one more in my kitchen before you arrived."

"Silly things," Amy repeated.

"It might have been a frivolous fight, or it might be related to the murder," said Heather.

She was lost in thought, considering who could have committed the crime, when she and Amy reached the twenty-four-hour dining hall. Heather

154

paused and read a sign on the door.

"I really don't want to eat any dining hall food," said Amy.

"And we wouldn't be able to anyway," said Heather. She pointed at the sign. "It says that it's closed."

"But it's supposed to be open twenty-four hours a day, right? Or is this just false advertising?"

Heather marched up to the door and knocked on it. A maintenance man opened the door and began what sounded like a rehearsed speech.

"This dining hall is closed while we repair the pipes, but the dining hall in Sandy Hall is open during meal hours, and there are extra vending machines at the dorm." He paused as he looked at Heather and Amy. "Do you work here? Or are you parents?"

"Neither," said Amy.

"We were just wondering about this dining hall being closed," said Heather.

"I know it is unfortunate because the kids love being able to come here at all hours," said the man. "But a pipe burst, and we're taking a look at the whole system. We need to make sure it's safe before we let people back in here. And food can't be prepared without working water."

"When did this happen?" asked Heather. "How long has it been closed for?"

"Three days now," said the man. "Hopefully, we'll be ready to open again in just a few more."

Heather thanked him and then headed away from the building.

"Do you know what this means?" asked Heather.

"The students might riot because they can't get their French fries at two a.m.?"

"It means that Mark and Tom were lying about where they were on the night of the murder."

***

Heather and Amy hurried over to confront Greg's friends. Freckly Tom was hiding his face, but Mark was trying to be aloof.

"So what if that dining hall is closed?" said Mark. "Maybe we were at another one?"

"You told us it was the twenty-four-hour dining hall that you were in," said Amy.

"And the other dining hall on campus is only open during meal hours," said Heather. "We checked. It closed at seven. You couldn't have been there from ten to midnight."

"I guess we got the day confused," said Mark. "It's no big deal."

"It is a big deal," said Amy. "Because this means that you lied to us about where you were during the murder. Maybe you were in that alley, killing your friend."

"No," said Tom. "We wouldn't hurt Greg."

"We heard that you argued with him that day," said Heather. "About going to the party."

"Because he had other plans with us," said Tom. "But we wouldn't kill him over it. He was our friend."

"We just wanted him to do what he said he would do with us," said Mark. "Instead of bailing on us to go to a lame party with his girlfriend."

"And what was it that you were supposed to do?" asked Amy. "It wasn't to go to the dining hall late at night."

"Mark?" Tom asked, turning to his friend.

"We just wanted to hang out," said Mark stubbornly. "That's it."

"Boys, someone was killed," Heather said, appealing to them. "I'm sure whatever your other secret is, it can't be worse than that. We want to find out what happened to your friend."

"We don't know," said Mark. "We were here together at the time he was killed. We ordered a pizza and got it here. Yeah. That's what happened. I confused what day we got pizza where. But we were here with our pie."

"Do you have a receipt?" asked Amy.

"I don't know where I put it," said Mark.

"What about the name of the pizza place?" Amy continued.

"I'm not sure," said Mark. "They all sound so much alike."

Heather realized that they weren't going to get much more information from them. They were being decidedly secretive about that night. She looked around the room to see if there were any clues and thought she might have found one in the trashcan. It wasn't a receipt from a pizza place. Instead, it was from Prankster's Palace.

"What are you doing?" Mark asked her suddenly.

"Just wasting my time talking to you," said Heather brightly. "If you do decide to tell us any more about what happened that night so we can figure out what happened to your friend, please contact us or the Key West Police."

"Until then, I'll just keep thinking of you as prime suspects," said Amy.

Chapter 14 – A Prank Discussion

After leaving Mark and Tom, Heather hurried to find a campus directory. She found the large sign and looked at the display. Amy was at her heels.

"They're up to something," said Amy, looking back toward the way they came. "But does it have anything to do with the murder? I bet they could find a cane to hit their friend with if they really wanted to."

"It's a possibility," said Heather, but she was still focused on the directory.

"I wish we could get them to talk."

164

"We might have better luck if we talk to them one-on-one," said Heather.

"True. Tom did look like he might crack. We'd just have to get them apart."

"But we might not need to," said Heather. "I want to check something out first."

"What?" asked Amy, now looking at the directory map too. "Are you trying to figure out how we ran in circles today?"

"I saw a receipt from Prankster's Palace in the garbage," Heather explained. "I think it had to be recent. And I think the boys planned more Halloween mischief than just what they did with the eggs at Mr. Rankle's."

"Like what?"

"I don't know exactly," Heather admitted. "But follow my train of thought for a second."

"All aboard," Amy joked.

"When the boys egged Mr. Rankle's store, they got rid of the cartons nearby."

"Right. At the taco place."

"I think that this might have been planned for something near their rooms. Something on campus."

Amy nodded. "They mentioned before that they wanted to impress people at school. Having it close by could be the way to do it. But what was it? And where?"

"Well, it sounded like they chose Mr. Rankle's shop as the place to vandalize because Mr. Rankle was short with Greg when he went shopping there one day," said Heather. "So, who on campus might he have wanted to seek revenge against too?"

"Professor Adler!" Amy exclaimed.

"Exactly," said Heather. "I didn't notice anything in his office when we questioned him. So I thought I'd look up where his classroom is."

"Great idea," said Amy. "Except for one thing."

"What's that?"

"We might be walking into a trap."

***

Heather and Amy walked into the classroom, feeling a bit uneasy. Heather carefully turned the lights on, and they looked around. It appeared to be an average classroom where about thirty students could attend instead of a larger lecture hall.

"I don't like this," said Amy. "And not just because it reminds me of being in school, but because I'm afraid something is going to jump out at me at any minute."

"It is creepy," said Heather. "But it's probably better that private investigators find it rather than the staff or students."

"What could it be?" asked Amy. "Something related to Halloween? Do you think vampire bats are going to come down and bite us? Or we'll be pelted with pumpkins?"

"I'm just hoping we find out what Mark and Tom were up to. Then we can determine if it's an alibi for where they were at the time of the murder, or if it was a motive to kill."

Amy took a step forward and then stopped. "Maybe we should just turn back? Maybe what they bought at Prankster's Palace was a cane, and they used it in the alley that night? We should check with the store."

"We're here. We should check here first," said Heather. "I thought you were dressed as a cat burglar this year. Not a 'fraidy cat."

"I'm the one who makes bad puns," Amy said with a pout.

However, then she did follow Heather farther into the room. They looked around. There didn't seem to be too many hiding places. This appeared to be a room that professors took turns teaching in and there weren't many personal touches.

"There's no closet for a monster to jump out from or to hide skeletons in," said Amy.

Heather checked the podium for signs that something could be hiding inside it, but it was empty.

She leaned against it and thought.

"If Greg, Tom, and Mark wanted to cause mischief in Professor Adler's class, they most likely wanted to target him and not the other students."

"I didn't see anything under any of the student desks anyway," Amy reported.

"There's not much here at the front of the classroom though," said Heather. "What could it be?"

Amy walked up to her friend and touched her arm. "Maybe we were wrong about their plan. Maybe they didn't do anything here. Or they were going to and got spooked."

Heather nodded. She accepted the wisdom of the words but still couldn't shake the feeling that something was going to happen in this room. She could feel it in her gut. But then, what was she missing?

"There's nothing hiding in the furniture, and there's nothing strange about the walls," said Heather. "What does that leave?"

"Maybe there's a beating heart under the floor," said Amy, looking for bumps in the ground.

Heather thought that would have been some very eerie Poe-inspired mischief indeed. As Amy looked down, she looked up. That was when she saw the dent in the paneled ceiling.

"You were close," said Heather. "But it's the opposite. There's something in the ceiling. Above the podium here."

They hurried to move a desk underneath it and then climbed up on it. They were able to find their balance and reach the proper height to examine the ceiling. Heather carefully removed the panel next to it so they could see what was weighing down the other section.

"What is it?" asked Heather.

Amy exhaled sharply. "I can see a timer."

Heather felt her blood run cold. Maybe this wasn't harmless mischief. "Is it a bomb?"

"Worse," said Amy, and Heather wondered how that could be.

"What is it?"

"Spiders!"

Chapter 15 – Motives

"If you thought there was a bomb there, you should have called us earlier," said Ryan. Heather could tell he was upset.

Ryan and Peters were examining the device in the ceiling that the P.I.s had just found. Amy was staying against the far wall so there was no chance that the rubber spiders could fall on her. Heather was keeping close to the detectives so she wouldn't miss anything, but it seemed like she was also being chided for her decision not to call in the police.

"I didn't think it was a bomb until after we saw it," said Heather. "I thought it was going to be a

Halloween prank. And that's what it was."

"It's a spider bomb," said Amy with a shiver. "So gross."

"They're just rubber," said Peters.

"Still gross," said Amy.

"I called you as soon as we had some information that seemed worthwhile," said Heather. "I know that you're still investigating the Mr. Rankle angle of the crime."

"I didn't mean to make it sound like I don't trust your detection methods," said Ryan. "I just worry

about you. Especially when
bombs are involved."

"Spider bomb," Amy repeated,
sounding nauseated.

"I understand," said Heather. "But
I think this was a good clue that
we found."

"It's never good to find spider
bombs," said Amy.

"This set up looks pretty simple,"
said Peters. "I bet I can
determine when it was set up
here."

"That would be great," said
Heather. "We know that Mark and
Tom set up this spider trick. My

guess is that is what they were doing the night that Greg was killed. They were angry that he was bailing on them to go to the party when they had planned on setting up this prank. Then, they didn't want to admit that's where they were that night because they didn't want to get in trouble. But this is all a theory until we have proof."

Peters examined the timer. "We can have the lab confirm that it can't be faked, but this looks like just a countdown timer to me. And it lists how much time has passed in the corner. Counting backward, this timer would have had to be placed here at eleven p.m. the night of the murder."

"It seems like your feeling that the reason Mark and Tom didn't tell us their real alibi was because they were setting this up was right," said Ryan. "Though it doesn't completely clear them. Because the murder could have happened close to midnight."

"I think this also gives someone else a stronger motive," said Heather. "And maybe he just might be willing to lend his cane to the police."

***

"I don't say that I'm busy for my health, you know," said Professor Adler when he saw the four investigators outside his office door. "I do have lots of work to do to prepare for my classes. And lots of assignments to grade."

"We're rather busy too," said Ryan good-naturedly. "We're looking into the death of a college student."

"Very well," Professor Adler said, allowing them into his office. "But I don't know what I could tell you now that I couldn't tell these ladies before."

"We've learned some new information," said Heather.

"Oh. Do you want me to tell you about another one of my

students? Which one of them has the psychological makeup to commit a crime like this?"

"No. It's about your involvement," said Amy.

"My involvement?" asked Professor Adler. "Didn't you speak to my wife? Didn't she confirm that I was home at the time?"

"I did speak to her," Peters said, piping up. "Just before we came here. She said that she was sure you were home all night."

"Then, there you have it," said Professor Adler.

"But she also said that she fell asleep reading a book around nine o'clock," said Peters. "So, you see, she wasn't awake to confirm you were there at the exact time we want to know about."

Professor Adler threw his hands up in the air. "Why would I want to murder one of my students?"

"Maybe it wasn't planned?" suggested Amy. "It started off as one of your psychological teachings, but then you lost your temper?"

"I don't lose my temper," the professor said, but his voice was beginning to rise.

"Or you found out about what Greg was planning to do the next time you taught your intro class," said Heather. "I would certainly be angry about that."

"I have no idea what you're talking about," said Professor Adler.

"Greg Chambers and a few of his friends rigged a device in your classroom that would have made hundreds of rubber spiders fall on you while you were standing at the podium," Ryan explained.

"Truly terrifying," Amy said as she imagined it.

"This is the first I've heard of that," said Professor Adler. "And I do hope that action is being taken against these individuals. The school won't allow for this sort of mischief to happen."

"Well, no action will be taken against Greg Chambers," said Heather. "Because somebody already decided to murder him."

"It wasn't me," said Professor Adler. "And, of course, I didn't mean punishment like that against the culprits. Still, a prank like that cannot be condoned."

"Maybe you found out about it and decided to teach Greg a lesson," said Amy. "Maybe he was bragging about his plan. We heard him gloat before."

"No," Professor Adler said firmly. "I did no such thing. I was preparing for my conference, and I didn't spend one moment of thought on Greg Chambers. I didn't know anything about his prank. And I would have reported it to the Dean if I had caught wind of it. I wouldn't have brutalized him in the streets."

"Do you mind if we take your cane to be analyzed in the lab?" asked Ryan. "It's consistent with the size of the murder weapon."

"I really don't like to be without it," Professor Adler said. "But if it will stop these irritating interrogations, I suppose I will surrender it. Then, you can get back to finding the real guilty party."

Heather stared at him as he handed the cane over to the detectives. She wasn't sure that they hadn't already found the real killer.

Chapter 16 – The Missing Clue

"Donut break!" Heather cried.

Her call was greeted with great glee, and everyone ran toward her to get a Candy Corn Donut. Her friends and family were helping her clean up, organize the furniture, and hang up decorations for the Halloween party the next day. Eva and Leila had come over, and though they teased that their senior bones couldn't handle manual labor, they were happy to hang up bat decorations. Lilly had been adding cling-ons to the windows and mirrors in the house. Amy was also helping and was adding some artistic touches to the centerpiece decorations.

Heather had let her friends have the more fun jobs and was doing the dusting herself. She was glad that she had a task to occupy her. She kept thinking about the case and was getting frustrated. She had promised Ethel that if Mr. Rankle were innocent, she would find the person who really committed the crime by Halloween. She wasn't sure that she was going to be able to keep this promise.

Heather watched as her friends and daughter enjoyed the donuts and tried to appreciate her snack as well. Her mind kept bringing up thoughts of the case and was overpowering her taste buds.

It was possible that Professor Adler was the killer, but then why had he agreed to turn over his cane? Was it because he was innocent? Or had Professor Adler only allowed the police to take the cane because he had done something to destroy any traces of blood on it after Heather and Amy went to talk to him? Was Mr. Rankle really the guilty one and was trying to avoid testing his cane altogether?

"You have that look on your face, dear," said Eva.

"Is something wrong?" asked Leila.

"I'm just thinking about the case," Heather admitted. "But I don't want to bring down the party mood."

"It's just party setup," Eva assured her.

"And if we can help, we'd love to," said Leila.

"That's right," said Lilly. "It's more important that you catch the bad guy than we hang the piñata early."

"I'm touched," Heather said.

"And talking with you about the case also means that we have a longer break and can eat more donuts," Amy teased.

Dave barked as if he agreed, and Cupcake moved closer to the group as well.

"All right," Heather said. "We'll try talking this case out. What we know is that Greg Chambers was killed slightly off campus between ten-thirty and midnight with a weapon resembling a cane."

"Like that Mr. Rankle's," said Leila.

"I don't think that's helping," said Eva, shushing her friend.

"No. It is," said Heather. "Because that's part of the possibility why Mr. Rankle could be the killer. Greg Chambers and his friends vandalized Sun and Fun Novelties. Mr. Rankle was angry about this, and he doesn't have an alibi."

"But do you think he did it?" asked Lilly.

"Not really," said Heather. "He may be unpleasant, but I don't think he's a murderer."

"Maybe you're right," said Amy. "If he was, he might have tried to silence me a long time ago."

"So, who are you other suspects?" asked Eva, reaching for another donut.

"Professor Adler seems like a strong possibility," said Heather. "He also has a cane that could be the murder weapon."

"Though his is only decorative," said Amy.

"He had trouble with Greg Chambers in class and insulted him. It's clear neither of them liked each other. And Greg and his friends were planning a prank on the professor."

"A terrible, terrible prank," said Amy. "With spiders."

"Professor Adler's alibi is also weak," said Heather. "But I don't know why Greg would agree to go toward that alley with him."

"Who else could it be?" asked Leila.

"Maybe his girlfriend," said Heather. "She was with him shortly before the murder because they went to a party together. But other girls who lived on her floor told us they saw her return home around ten-thirty."

"Yeah. She was complaining about her witch costume getting spilled on," said Amy.

"And his friends Tom or Mark might also have done it," said Heather. "They did have a fight about the party earlier. And the time that the prank—"

"The spider bomb," said Amy.

"Was set," Heather continued, "doesn't completely prove their innocence. They might have set it and then met Greg and murdered him."

"Or only one of them did it," said Amy. "Maybe one set the spider bomb while the other killed Greg out of rage. The other friend is covering because he doesn't want to lose two of his friends."

"Good point," said Heather. "And it also could have been someone else at the party who committed the murder. We're just not sure who else was there right now because everyone was in costume. We'll have to find another witness to tell us who more of the guests were."

"This certainly does seem like a pickle," said Eva.

"Does anyone jump out at you as the killer?" asked Leila.

"I'm just not sure," said Heather. "Maybe I should just get back to cleaning. Maybe the distraction will actually help me to think more clearly."

"Whatever you need, dear," said Eva.

"Of course, I think I need another donut," said Leila.

Heather told them all to help themselves. She decided that she had finished dusting for the day and could move on to the floors. She picked up the broom but then froze. She stared at it.

"The broom!"

"Do you want me to sweep?" asked Amy.

"No. I mean, yes, we should sweep before the party. But I

think I figured out the case. I'm pretty sure I know who did it. I just need to confirm something with the bracelet-makers. And then figure out how to prove it all."

"At least I don't have to keep cleaning," Amy joked. "Let's go catch the killer!"

Chapter 17 – Catching the Killer

"Are we almost there?" asked Amy.

"Be quiet," Heather reminded her. "We don't want the killer to know we're here."

Amy nodded and mimed zipping up her lips. Heather kept her eyes on the culprit, hoping they would be led straight to the evidence she wanted.

She watched as Georgia looked around to make sure she wasn't being followed, and thankfully missed the investigators in their hiding places. They were near the edge of campus before they would have reached the alleyway. Georgia walked up to a business's dumpster. She opened the lid and peered inside. After nodding in satisfaction, she began to walk away. However, her path was soon blocked by two detectives and two P.I.s.

"What are you doing here?" Georgia asked.

"The same thing as you," Amy quipped. "Looking for a murder weapon."

"What?" asked Georgia. "That's not what I was doing."

"So, we won't find what killed Greg Chambers inside that dumpster?" asked Heather.

"Well, I have no idea about that," Georgia said, crossing her arms. "I was just checking to make sure that no recyclables had been placed in there. You have to keep trash and recycling separate. Sometimes the students here forget that."

"Georgia, as soon as we look in there, we're going to be able to prove that you killed Greg," said Heather. "Do you have anything that you want to tell the detectives?"

"Why would I kill my boyfriend?" Georgia protested. "I loved him."

"We heard that you had been fighting with him," said Amy. "And maybe you didn't plan on killing him. Maybe it just escalated. And you happened to be carrying the weapon with you. Maybe he was even the one who spilled the drink on you, and you were mad."

"But what weapon did I have?"

"We got sidetracked when we were told that the weapon resembled a cane," said Heather. "We got it stuck in our minds because it was the example and it did seem like the most likely item that someone would be carrying around with him."

"Like Mr. Rankle or Professor Alder," said Amy.

"But that's not what was used. It was a broom that killed him. Struck with a lot of angry force repeatedly. And it was your witch's broom that you used."

Georgia just shook her head.

"It didn't occur to me before because a witch's costume doesn't necessarily need a broom as part of it. You had the wig and hat," said Heather. "But then I remembered how one of the girls on your floor described you before you left. That you looked ready to fly off into the night. Why would she use that description? She could have said that you looked ready to cast a spell or cackle. But she said fly because she remembered seeing you with a broom. We just confirmed it with her. Jess saw you leave the dorm with a broom as part of your costume."

"And Casey saw that you didn't have it when you returned," said Amy.

"We were starting to rely on you for the timeline of events," said Heather. "But you had an opportunity to kill Greg Chambers and then return to your room, pretending that nothing was bothering you more than a spill on your costume."

"And you used that as an excuse so you could wash it right away," said Amy. "You wanted to get all the blood off it too."

Detective Peters walked toward the dumpster.

"Wait," said Georgia. "You tricked me."

"After we spoke to the girls on your floor, we did leave them with the rumor that the police just found what they believed to be the murder weapon," said Heather. "It seems that you wanted to find out whether they really had recovered it."

"Instead, you led us right to it," said Amy.

Georgia opened and closed her mouth several times, but nothing came out. Peters opened the lid to the dumpster and looked inside.

"There is a broom there," he reported. "And I think there are still drops of blood that weren't cleaned off on it too."

"It's not fair," Georgia cried.

"What's not?" asked Amy. "You killed somebody, and we found the weapon."

"I didn't mean to kill him. I just wanted to hurt him," said Georgia. "He made me so mad. We had been having some problems. I didn't feel like he was taking me seriously and I was supposed to be his girlfriend. That's why I insisted we go to that party that night. He tried to tell me that he had plans with his friends, but I made him go to the party with me. And I still felt like he was ignoring me then! I grabbed his arm so he'd pay more attention to me and he spilled a drink all over my dress. I was furious. He didn't even seem sorry."

"So, you hit him?" Heather suggested.

"We did fight about leaving. He told me just to go home if I was so upset. He said he wanted to stay at the party until it was time to meet his friends. They were up to some prank. And I almost did walk home," said Georgia. "But then I went back and I told him that I wanted to make up. We walked away from campus because the music was so loud. But then he didn't apologize. I got so mad I just started hitting him. Again and again. And then I realized how badly I hurt him. I panicked and tried to hide the broom and come up with a cover story. I figured people at the party wouldn't remember exactly what time some freshmen left... I thought I could get away with it..."

"We're going to have to take you to the station now," said Ryan.

Georgia just whimpered. She allowed Ryan and Detective Peters to lead her away. Heather and Amy volunteered to watch the dumpster until the evidence could be properly collected.

"I'm glad I was able to keep my promise to Ethel to find the real killer before Halloween," said

Heather. "I'm looking forward to seeing Mr. Rankle all dressed up."

"And I'm excited to see you dressed up," said Amy. "Now that I know what the costume is."

"What?" asked Heather. "How did you find out?"

"I used all my investigative prowess," said Amy. "And I contacted Imelda, who is making the costumes, and asked her!"

Chapter 18 – Happy Halloween

"This is a great party, Mom," Lilly said, taking a break from the festivities as a mummy to talk to her. "I'm almost disappointed it has to stop so we can go trick-or-treating."

"That will be just as much fun too," said Heather. "Now, why don't you gather everyone so we can break the monster piñata?"

Lilly smiled and said, "That's a boo-tiful idea."

She hurried off to gather her friends. Heather stood to the side, looking majestic. Ryan walked up to her and kissed her hand.

"M'lady," he said, grinning.

"M'lord," she said back.

They were dressed as a king and queen for the evening. She was afraid that the costumes might be too much and that she would be trying to look too much like "the boss" at work. However, after running around so much catching killers and getting flour in her hair in the kitchen, she wanted an excuse to dress up lavishly.

She had to admit that Ryan looked pretty handsome as a king too.

Though the best costumes she had seen of the night had been Mr. Rankle and Ethel's. They had stopped by before their cruise. It was strange to see them looking so out of character by dressing up. Mr. Rankle also did something else out of character and thanked Heather for clearing his name. They had even shaken hands.

Dave barked, and Heather reached down to pet him. He was dressed like a bumblebee and seemed to be announcing that he was not being given enough treats during the party. Cupcake was dressed like a ladybug and was climbing up the bookcases to get a better view of the piñata.

"It seems like everyone is having a great time," said Ryan.

"I'm so glad for Lilly," said Heather.

"And the fun doesn't end after the piñata is broken and the last apple is bobbed," said Ryan. "Because then we'll go out trick-or-treating."

"Did we hear trick-or-treating?" asked Leila, rushing over toward them. She was dressed up as a scarecrow.

Eva soon came over too, dressed as the tinman. "Because we'd love to get some donuts as treats."

"There should be some more Candy Corn Donuts in the kitchen," said Heather. "And you can give some to Vincent as well."

Eva smiled. "My beau will be joining us as the cowardly lion soon enough. After this party, we're headed to one at the senior center."

"But we'll be back to help with Lilly's candy tonight," Leila said with a wink.

They headed off toward the kitchen, but Heather soon saw

some other friends. Amy and Jamie walked over in their cat burglar costumes with cups of apple cider.

"Great costume choice," said Jamie. "And I can't believe we didn't guess it when we were given the clue that it was majestic."

"That's because we didn't think of it as a costume," said Amy.

"What?" asked Heather.

"Well," Amy explained. "Heather already is the Queen of Clues!"

Heather laughed. Then it was time to start the piñata game with the kids. She smiled contentedly as Lilly, the mummy, and Chelsea, the vampire, led their friends to the proper spot. It was a very happy Halloween this year.

The End.

A letter from the Author

To each and every one of my Amazing readers: I hope you enjoyed this story as much as I enjoyed writing it. Let me know what you think by leaving a review!

Stay Curious,
Susan Gillard

Made in the USA
Coppell, TX
01 September 2021

61642003R00125